T0145057

Max Goes Hunting

written and illustrated by

Elliott Gilbert

Max Goes Hunting

written and illustrated by
Elliott Gilbert

To order additional copies of this book, contact:
Xlibris
844-714-8691
www.Xlibris.com
Orders@Xlibris.com

ISBN: Softcover   978-1-6698-0290-7
       Hardcover   978-1-6698-0289-1
       EBook   978-1-6698-0288-4

Library of Congress Control Number: 2021924923

Print information available on the last page.

Rev. date: 12/08/2021

For Eva, Nathan, Amanda, Gabriel, and Vanessa.

Max Marten was only three weeks old with soft cuddly fur, and he still wobbled when he walked. So his mother would bring him pieces of meat or fruit and nuts. "Eat what I bring you so you can learn to run quickly and grow up healthy!" she would say.

Sometimes his mother would come back with a fish in her mouth that was almost as long as she was. Max and his young brothers and sisters would eat up the whole thing.

One day when Max was about three months old, his father said: "Son, you're now old enough to learn how to feed yourself. Come with your mom and me and we'll show you how." They went into the woods where the high grass hid them and they could look for prey.

"Look," whispered his mother, "There's a rabbit! Now you must be very quiet and patient. If you are too noisy, you'll frighten the rabbit away before we can catch it!"

4

Max watched as his mother crawled slowly closer and closer to the unsuspecting rabbit. "It's very fast," his father said quietly, "so we must come as close as possible before it sees us."

Slowly, slowly, Max and his parents crawled through the tall grass, their bellies hugging the ground, eyes intent on their prey. They were just a few feet away when Max's parents froze. The rabbit's nose twitched; its ears were straight up and it was breathing hard. Then off it went!

With its powerful rear legs, the rabbit bounded over the grass, up and down, like a huge super-fast grasshopper. Max struggled to keep up with the chase, for he hadn't yet developed much speed. But it didn't matter because Max's mother and father were much faster. Suddenly there was a squeal, and his mother had the rabbit between her sharp teeth. What a delicious dinner everyone had later! And there was plenty for all.

Now the sun sank slowly into the trees, and the forest came alive with chattering crickets and bird songs. All the marten cubs were asleep except Max. "It's time for you to hunt alone" his parent told him. "You are old enough now. Besides, we've taught you all we know, and we're not getting any younger." Max was eager to show his hunting skills the next day, for it would prove how grown up he was. He was so excited he had a hard time sleeping that night.

Early the next morning, Max was already deep in the forest, and by midday was getting very hungry, for he had still seen no food. He remained quiet and moved slowly, just as his parents had. He listened, sniffed, and looked everywhere for signs of movement.

He didn't have to wait much longer. "Chirp chirp," he heard. He scampered over to its source and saw a little sparrow that had fallen from its nest. Its frightened mother was nearby, fluttering her wings and moving protectively about her baby.

"You may eat me, but please don't eat my baby!" she pleaded. "Surely I would make a more satisfying meal."

Max hesitated. The little sparrow was helpless. It had just been hatched and could not yet see or move. "I'm so hungry, but how can I eat this baby or her mother?" he thought. He turned away and ran back into the woods.

Max decided to climb a tree in order to observe where he might yet find a meal. He sat motionless in the branches, until he noticed movement in the bushes below. Suddenly, out hopped a little white rabbit! In a flash, Max sprang from his branch and in two leaps, overtook him.

"Don't eat me!" the rabbit pleaded. It was very tiny; it's eyes were wide open and it was trembling from head to toe. As Max held the rabbit between his paws, he realized how small indeed it was.

"Must be a baby," he told himself, as he released his grip and the little rabbit bounded away.

Soon Max was in thick grass, resting and wondering what to do next, when he felt something move under his right paw. He lifted it, and there was a mouse! It tried to scurry away, but faster than you can count to three, Max had him under his paw again. "For the sake of all my children, please don't eat me!" squeaked the mouse. And since Max came from a large family himself, he understood how helpless that family of mice would be without its parent. Besides, it wasn't much of a meal. He lifted his paw and the mouse disappeared into the dark grass.

Now it was too dark in the forest to do anything but return home. And Max was hungrier than ever, so hungry he would have eaten grass. It had been a windy day and he noticed a few apples that had fallen from its tree to the ground. Desperately Max snatched them and swallowed them almost whole. Not bad! he thought, as he smacked his lips. They were so tasty he looked for more, and found peaches that had also fallen from their tree.

Delicious! Max then remembered a nearby garden and quietly helped himself to grapes, nuts, berries, cherries, even lettuce and string beans—it was all SO good!

As he neared the trees where his family lived, his brothers and sisters and parents gathered around him.

"Where have you been?" asked his father.

"Yes, where *have* you been?" repeated his brothers and sisters.

"I was hunting for my dinner," replied Max.

"You certainly took a long time about it," his father said.

"Have you had anything to eat?" asked his mother.

"Oh yes," said Max, "First, I had a delicious rabbit. Then I caught and ate a few sparrows. And then later for a snack, a mouse."

"Why didn't you bring anything back for us?" cried his younger brothers and sisters.

"I meant to," replied Max, "but I was tired and so far away from home that I was afraid I wouldn't make it back." And then he said, "Mom, I'm so tired, I think I'll go to bed now."

"You poor dear," said his mother.

Max felt terrible about being untruthful. He realized how much his family had expected him to be a skilled hunter, but he simply could not hurt those innocent little creatures.

That night, as Max slept, he dreamed about his next meals from the forest. He could hardly wait until morning.

ELLIOTT GILBERT has illustrated and written other children's picture books, including *A Cat Story, Mittens in May* by Maxine Kumin, and *The Best Loved Doll* by Rebecca Caudill. His paintings have been exhibited in many galleries, and won numerous awards. Examples of his work can be seen on his website, elliottgilbert.com. He lives with his wife in Hoboken, New Jersey.

Printed in the United States
by Baker & Taylor Publisher Services